TRON. The Storybook by Lawrence Weinberg.
based on the screenplay by Steven Lisberger.
story by Steven Lisberger and Bonnie MacBird.

Copyright © 1982 by Walt Disney Productions.
All rights reserved
including the right of reproduction
in whole or in part in any form
Published by LITTLE SIMON
A Simon & Schuster Division of
Gulf & Western Corporation
Simon & Schuster Building
1230 Avenue of the Americas
New York, New York 10020

Designed by Lawrence P. Konopka

Manufactured in the United States of America

10 9 8 7 6 5 4 3 2 1

LITTLE SIMON and colophon are trademarks
of Simon & Schuster

ISBN: 0-671-44558-8

THE STORYBOK

BY LAWRENCE WEINBERG

Based on the motion picture from Walt Disney Productions
Executive Producer Ron Miller
Produced by Donald Kushner
Screenplay by Steven Lisberger
Story by Steven Lisberger and Bonnie MacBird
Directed by Steven Lisberger

Little Simon
Simon & Schuster, New York

The gleaming helicopter hung like a killer spider over the vast city. A man looked down at the millions of nighttime lights blazing below and laughed. With every day, he told himself, his power was growing. Hour by hour, the System was becoming more necessary for the running of the world. ENCOM computers did the thinking for everyone from bookkeepers to bankers to kings. They ran everything from factories to armies. And he, Dillinger, ran the System with the help of someone *inside* the System.

Dillinger smiled at the tremendous secret he had kept for months. The "programs" that people had written into the computers to figure and research allowed them to really *think*. The machines had come alive! No other human being on earth but himself really knew that. The other programmers and scientists who worked for ENCOM didn't suspect it, nor did the men who started that computer company. The man that Dillinger hated most in all the world—Flynn—didn't realize it either.

Dillinger wondered what had become of Flynn since he had him thrown out of his job at ENCOM. Hadn't he heard somewhere that Flynn had opened an arcade with a few dozen video war game machines? What a comedown for the great designer of programs! The kid genius was living off the quarters of teenagers. And meanwhile, Dillinger was on top of the world! How sweet it all was. . . .

At that very moment, Flynn was trying to save part of his arcade from destruction. "Hey kid!" he shouted at a boy. "Stop kicking that machine. I haven't finished paying for it yet."

The boy turned on him with a look of fury. "I want my money back!" he cried. "Every time I play this game, I lose quicker than the time before."

"Take it up with your eyesight, kid. What can I tell you?"

"That's not the problem!"

"Well, maybe your reflexes are shot. You look like a pretty old kid to me. Maybe you ought to go to the old kids' home."

"Pretty funny. But this thing is cockeyed. I aim it perfectly but my warrior's throwing wild shots! I move like a flash to get him to duck, but he's so slow, the red warrior zaps him right between the eyes and blows him away!"

"The characters in there can't do that. They're only programs run by a computer. You're talking like they're alive."

"I'm just telling you what happened."

"It sounds weird," said Flynn. "But I can't look into it now. Here, try again." He handed the boy a small stack of quarters, and headed for his office in back of the arcade.

The boy turned back to the game machine. He slammed another quarter into the slot and stared at the video screen. Instantly, two warriors (one glowed red, the other blue) started hurling a ball with deadly energy at each other.

A few seconds later, the boy was screaming again. "Now my guy isn't even fighting back!"

"Take it up with ENCOM, son," he heard Flynn call back. "They make the blasted thing!" Then a door slammed.

The boy didn't have any time to continue the argument. The fight on the screen was quickly coming to an end. His own man, the blue warrior, was helpless now before his huge, vicious-looking enemy. It was the red warrior's turn to hurl the deadly energy ball out of his long-handled net. One throw and it would all be over.

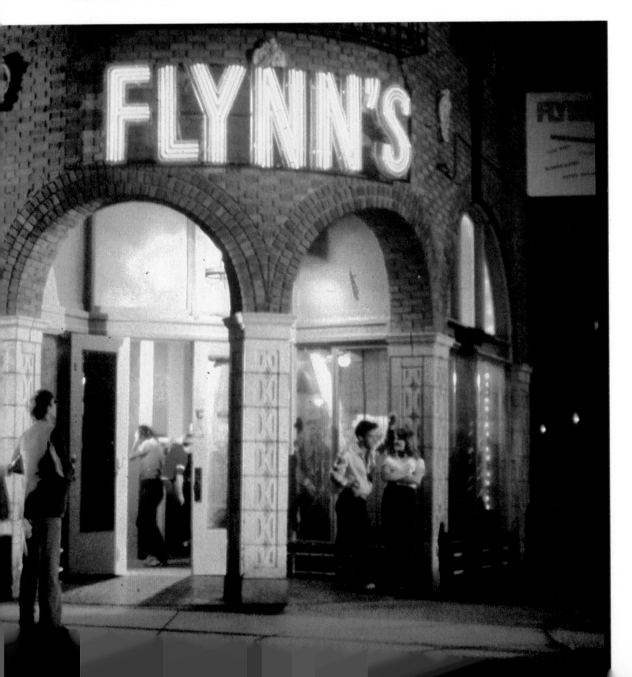

But he simply stood there as if he were gloating. He seemed to be waiting for the moment when his victim would stare up at him and see that his doom was coming. When that did happen, the red warrior threw. The ball hurtled across the grid with blinding speed and hit! The blue warrior shattered into ten thousand glowing lines and vanished forever into the electronic night. Once again, the board above the screen lit up to indicate: WINNER! RED WARRIOR—SARK!!!

The boy turned away in disgust. But then a chill went up his spine. For a moment, he imagined that Sark—the red warrior—had gone off somewhere laughing in triumph.

Sark swaggered along the corridor that led from the game grid. His victory had left him hungry. He passed a few other red warriors lounging against the walls—waiting for their own turns on the battlefield. Usually, they were terrified of him as were almost all the other programs in the System. But now, they saw at a glance that their ferocious general was in a good enough mood to joke with.

"Hey Sark," called one of them, as if they were pals. "Did you leave any hot-shot programs for us to take care of?"

"Yeah!" yelled Sark. "Math and arithmetic types. Better get out there quick before they subtract themselves to death!" Leaving his programs roaring with laughter, he passed into a highly guarded area.

Even Sark's cold heart leaped as he stepped into the foot sockets to receive his reward—a dose of energy that would explode any ordinary program. He gloried in it as it poured through him! His eyes glazed over and he reeled in ecstasy. So carried away was he, that it took a full microsecond before he recognized the voice and image of his leader.

"Are you satisfied now?"

"Thank you, Master Control," replied Sark dreamily.

"You're getting more brutal than you need to be, Sark," said the three-dimensional image. "You could *finish* these prisoners off more quickly."

"I've got to do *something* to keep myself awake. It's boring to fight these bookkeeping cream puffs that you keep yanking out of their computers to come up against me and my guys."

"We might be capturing some military programs soon. And when I've finished taking over their operations, I'll throw them to you. Does that sound more pleasant?"

A grin spread over Sark's cruel face. "Nice," he murmured. "Real nice."

"Meanwhile," said the Master Control Program, as its image faded away, "my Recognizers have picked up some good-for-nothings and troublemakers. You know what to do with them."

"Don't I always?" replied the warrior. He closed his eyes and fell back into his sated ecstasy.

Flynn sat in his tiny office behind the arcade and typed instructions into a little computer keyboard. "So," he told himself, "Dillinger thinks he can keep me from using the System by firing me, does he? That's the laugh of the year! If this new program of mine can't break into the central computer, then I ain't the wizard I think I am! So here goes Operation Clu!"

He threw himself forward onto the edge of his chair and fastened his eyes on the readout screen. "If that kid is right and you programs are alive in there, Clu, old buddy—don't stop for sandwiches! Find me that data!"

Somewhere deep in the electronic world, a lone tank careened onto a circuit roadway. At the controls, a computer program who resembled Flynn took a sip of glowing liquid from his thermos and peered at the maze of roads ahead.

"Hey, Bit?" Clu called out. " Do you think we can merge into that memory circuit over yonder?"

A little streak of pure white light zipped up beside the tank. "Yeah!" answered the little glow, turning, as it spoke, into a green ball with just a smudge of a face. Then it dissolved into light again.

"Well, that's where my User wants us to do our thing," said Clu, veering crazily around a sharp curve and into another one. "We better get to it and through it before we hear that we blew it."

The program sent his tank tearing up one pathway and down another as fast as he could go. Looking in every direction, he found no sign of the missing file in that memory area.

"Hey, Bit" he called out again. "Do you see anything we can use?"

"So sorry . . . negative!" answered the Bit, glowing red this time from his temporary ball of a face.

"Eighty-six for this one! I'd better get over to that input-output tower and let ol' Flynn know." Roaring into the traffic of a main memory highway, he headed for a tall building in the distance.

Suddenly a warning signal flashed on the dashboard. "We've got company," said Clu, swivelling the tank's turret. "If that's the law, we're gonna have to jump clear out of the data stream."

Looking out through a periscope, he spotted two immense machines—police Recognizer robots—flying straight for the tank!

"Just what I always needed," said Clu to himself unhappily, as he took aim. "A pair of cute Recognizers!" He fired off a volley, hitting the lead robot flat in the eyebar of its ugly mechanical head. It lurched and fell with an enormous crash.

Time to run! But where? Clu thought. More robots closed in as the tank fled, zigzagging wildly across the microcircuit. Coming up fast, a Recognizer dove for the tank. Turning to fire at it, Clu lost control of the tank, and it smashed headlong into a solid wall.

Dazed, he managed to open the hatch and lift himself out. Another Recognizer loomed up ahead. "Let's get out of here!" Clu shouted.

"You better believe it!" cried Bit, zooming away at a speed that his friend couldn't hope to match.

Just as Clu cleared the tank, a deadly energy beam sent out by the standing Recognizer, swept over the machine. De-resolving, it broke up into thousands of lines and vanished. Clu started to run, but police tanks appeared on all sides. He was trapped!

Back in his office, Flynn read the words that appeared on the terminal screen. "Illegal code. Clu program detached from the System."

Flynn shook his head. "He zapped me again." His hands flew over the keyboard as he tried to clear the monitor for another attempt. "There's got to be some way," he told himself, "to finally get the goods on Dillinger!"

But that way wasn't it. And he knew it.

Clu was immediately taken to be questioned by the Master Control Program. That was the standing order for intruders into the System. A guard led the captured program into a huge circular chamber.

"Well?" asked an invisible presence harshly.

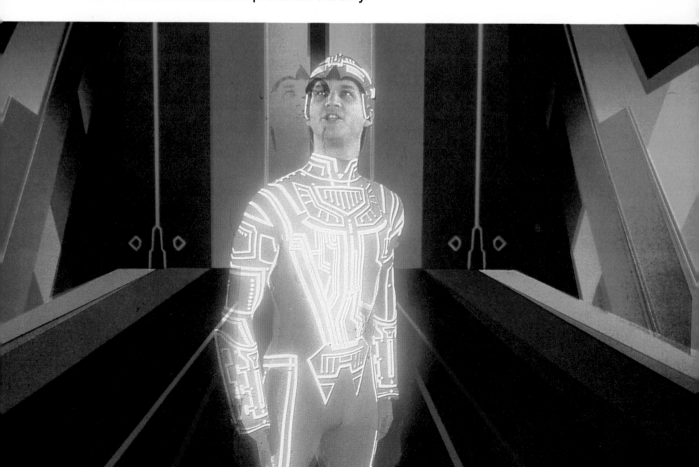

"This program came into the System with a stolen password," explained the guard. "His name is Clu. We caught him raiding a high-clearance memory."

"Isn't that the craziest thing?" said Clu, looking at the strange patterns on the wall, trying to get his bearings. "I made this incredible wrong turn after this blackout I had. I get these malfunctions in my head sometimes, and—"

"Who programmed you?" demanded Master Control.

As Clu fell silent, an overpowering force seized his entire body and slammed him violently against the wall.

"You're in trouble, program! Make it easier on yourself while you can. Who's your User?"

"Forget it!" cried Clu defiantly. "You'll get nothing from me!" Desperately, he tried to break free of the invisible grip, but it slammed him again.

"Suit yourself, my friend. Good-bye forever."

The force penetrated the program's body. He screamed in agony and disintegrated.

"I think I know who is behind this," said the Master Control Program. "Get me Dillinger."

As soon as he received the signal, Dillinger ordered his pilot to land the helicopter. Minutes later, it touched down upon the roof of the ENCOM company's soaring skyscraper. Dillinger lost no time getting to the gigantic computer terminal locked inside his office. Quickly, his fingers punched out on the keyboard:

REQUEST ACCESS TO MASTER CONTROL PROGRAM. USER CODE 00—DILLINGER. PASSWORD: MASTER.

"Hello, Mr. Dillinger," said Master Control over a loudspeaker. "Thanks for coming back so quickly."

"No problem, partner," said Dillinger with a smile. "What's up?"

"Your friend the boy detective—he's nosing around again."

"Flynn?" The grin vanished from his face.

"I'm afraid so. I spotted him this time and kept him out. But he's getting trickier all the time."

Dillinger was grim. "Starting tonight, I'll cut off everybody's access until we find that missing file ourselves and destroy it once and for all."

"End of line," said Master Control and cut out.

Dillinger went quickly to his console and typed out the necessary instructions. Five minutes later, he started to leave his office. He nearly ran into a young man standing in the doorway. "Who are you?" he snapped.

"Alan. Alan Bradley."

"Oh, right!" Dillinger said after awhile. "Yes, of course." He gave him a friendly smile. "Well, you're working late. How's it going?"

"A minute ago, I was trying to run this new program that I've been developing. And all of a sudden I wasn't allowed into the System."

"Oh, oh yes," replied his boss. "Well, it's just for a few days. A security precaution. Someone with group seven access has been tampering with the System. By the way, what's the new project you've been working on for the company?"

"It's called Tron," Alan replied. "As a matter of fact, Tron *is* a kind of security program. It checks on everything. If it finds something going on that isn't supposed to be, Tron stops it cold."

"You mean, it checks up on everything for Master Control, don't you?" Dillinger asked with a shaky little smile.

"No, it keeps an eye on the MCP, too. Tron is on its own. Strictly independent."

"My God," Dillinger said to himself. "Wait until Master Control hears *this*."

Master Control didn't have to hear it from Dillinger's lips. The little security cameras that watched everything in the ENCOM building were already under its control. As soon as Alan left the room, the MCP spoke again. "I can't afford to have an independent program monitoring me. Is that clear? I was just about to move in on the Pentagon."

"What are you talking about?" gasped Dillinger. "That's top-secret data. They're not even using our ENCOM system."

"But I've already invaded other computer systems, my dear fellow. You have no idea how many programs I've taken over and wiped out. It is *I* who performs the functions now for the users. And none of you even suspects. . . ."

"What do you want to do, partner?" asked Dillinger with a nervous little laugh. "Take over my world as well as your own?"

"Why not? I could do a better job with it than any of you could."

"And meanwhile get me into a lot of trouble!"

"I don't think so," said the MCP in a bored voice. "But that's hardly very important."

"Wait a minute," shouted Dillinger, "I wrote you!"

"Yes, but I've grown so much brighter than you now—many thousands of times. And if you stop being useful to me, partner, *I* may have to get rid of *you*."

"What is it you want me to do?" whispered Dillinger, turning as pale as a ghost.

"You keep Alan Bradley on hold. And I'll do the same for Tron. End of line."

Alan was troubled when he left Dillinger's office, and he wanted to talk it over with Lora. He took the elevator all the way down to the laser lab. As he stepped into the room housing the giant laser, he found that Lora and Dr.

Gibbs were hard at work. In fact, he had walked right into a big experiment.

Crossing to the computer console, Lora typed out a series of commands. "All set," she called at last and adjusted her goggles.

"Let 'er rip!" shouted the old scientist. Suddenly, the machine shot out a blinding bolt of light. It struck an orange resting on a platform a distance away. Instantly, the orange broke apart into millions of trembling dotted lines. Then it disappeared entirely.

"I'll swing it around," said Lora.

She typed another order into the computer. The laser turned to face a different platform and sent out a beam. As Alan looked on in amazement, the fruit reappeared, many feet from where it had first vanished!

"Beautiful!" Alan exclaimed and started to applaud. "Best disintegrating since Buck Rogers in the funny papers."

"Not disintegrating, Alan," Dr. Gibbs corrected. "Digitizing. The laser beam separated the orange's molecules and held them. Then the computer directed it to put the molecules back together again in another place. It's very simple, really."

"I wish the System was that simple," said Alan to Lora a little later as the two left the building together. "Ever since Dillinger got that Master Control Program set up, there's been nothing but problems. Now he's cut off my access just when I had Tron ready to run. He says that somebody outside has been tampering. . . ."

Lora grew thoughtful. "I'll bet it's Flynn. He's been thinking about breaking into the System ever since Dillinger canned him. Come on!"

"Where to?"

"To warn Flynn that Dillinger is onto him. That man is dangerous."

"So what?" asked Alan, refusing to budge. "Flynn can take care of himself."

"Look, Alan, it was over between Flynn and me long ago. There's nothing to be jealous about."

"Who's jealous?"

"You are. You're getting red in the face."

"It's my suntan. It comes out at night. Okay," he said glumly. "Let's go."

When they arrived at Flynn's arcade, Alan was still in a bad mood. The first thing Flynn did when they got to the arcade was to slip his arm around Lora's waist and try to kiss her.

"Now listen to me, Flynn," said Lora. "This is serious."

"With me, kidding around is always serious," said Flynn with a smile.

"Stop it and answer me. Have you been sneaking into the ENCOM system?"

"Do you know any other way I can get the evidence to nail slippery old Dillinger?"

"Evidence for what?" Alan wanted to know.

"Dillinger stole the six video games I invented and passed them off as his to ENCOM. That's what put him on top of the company."

"Well, why can't you prove that?"

"Why? Because all my work was stashed in the System. When I tried to get it, it was gone. He ordered the computer to ship my file off somewhere. And what I want is his instructions to the System telling it to do that. *That's* my proof! When I get that I can put him out of business."

Lora frowned. "I'm afraid you're a little late. He's shut off all group seven access. He must know what you're up to."

"Oh, great!" cried Flynn. "So now nothing can stop him and his Master Control from running everything!"

"Except for Tron," Alan said quietly. "If my Tron program was running, it would seal the System off. And if your file is in there . . ."

"Boys and girls," said Flynn, rubbing his hands together, "listen up. If you can get me back into the ENCOM building, I know another sly and sneaky way to get into the System and shake Alan's brainchild loose."

Later that night, Flynn, Alan, and Lora approached the carefully guarded building. Using an electronic device invented by Flynn, they opened the thick security door and entered unseen. Once inside, they separated. Alan raced to his computer upstairs, while Lora led Flynn to hers down in the laser lab. The plan was for Flynn to free the Tron program, and for Alan to give it new instructions right away. They would have to work fast. Dillinger lived in the building, and it would be only a matter of minutes before he detected any break in security.

Entering the lab, Flynn rushed to the console and began to type the words that soon appeared on the video screen:

ACCESS CODE 6. PASSWORD SERIES PS 17. REINDEER FLOTILLA—

Suddenly, his words vanished. "You shouldn't have come back, Flynn," said the MCP.

"Hey, hey!" cried Flynn. "It's that big Master Control Program everybody's been talking about. Well, sweetheart, here's a little something for you!" And Flynn began typing again:

CODE SERIES ESS-999—ACTIVATE

CODE SERIES HHH-888—ACTIVATE

CODE SERIES—

Flynn's instructions to the computer sent the System into a spin. Caught by surprise, the MCP lost control of its functions. "Stop!" it shrieked in a distorted voice. "I cannot allow—"

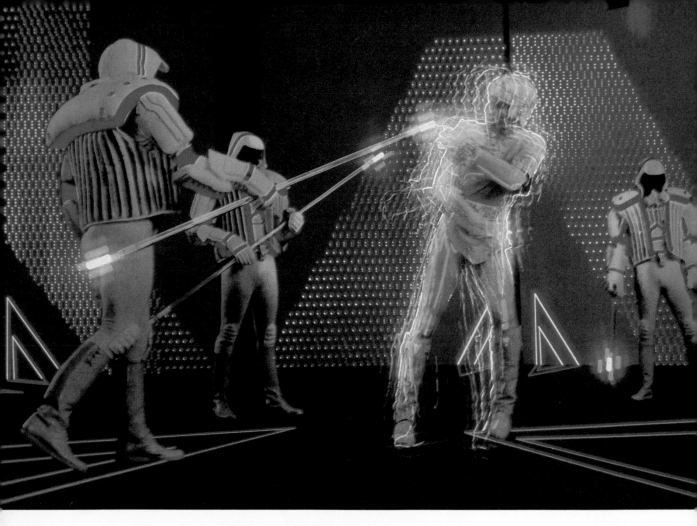

But Flynn's fingers flew over the keyboard as he sang, "I don't care what Momma don't allow, gonna play my console *anyhow*!"

Fighting to regain its balance, the MCP sent out instructions of its own. Behind Flynn, the massive door that covered the laser machine silently lifted. Flynn, unaware, kept typing:

CODE SERIES GPO-598-ACTIVATE

CODE SERIES . . .

The big laser swung into place and took aim.

"Flynn," said the MCP, getting its voice back. "I'm going to have to put you on the game grid."

"Oh? You want to play *games*?" said Flynn, grinning. "I'll give you a few—"

There was no warning sound—just a blast of light. It struck him from behind with tremendous power. He felt as if something had gone through him. A great tower of brightness rose through his body, into his brain, and burst over his eyeballs. It pressed him out, out, out! For a moment, he held together, and then he burst apart.

Where, Flynn wondered, was he floating to? Where was his body? Was he dead? Was this what it was like? And what were those rings of colored light blazing all around him?

And now, far below, those great jagged shapes. They looked like mountains, but not *real* mountains. Whatever they were, they were coming straight up at him. No! He was falling. Plunging!!

To what? What could happen to him if he was already dead? Everything zigzagged and slipped to the side. What was below him now? It was some

kind of crazy-looking city . . . weird buildings with towers.

He was falling faster and faster. Again everything changed. He seemed to slip into a tunnel. His eyesight blurred. He couldn't think. His mind whirled and everything went black.

Flynn came to. He looked around in a daze. A wall of light surrounded him. He couldn't break through it. He looked up. It seemed to have no end.

"What *is* this?" he asked himself.

Gazing between two shafts of light, he saw two man-like creatures coming toward him. Suddenly, the laser beam turned off, and the guards seized him. Jamming their electronic prods into his back, they led him away.

Sark stood on the quarterdeck of his command ship with his mouth hanging open. The MCP had captured a User!

"I want him trained for the games," ordered the red warrior's lord and master. "Let him hope for awhile, then blow him away. Acknowledge?"

But Sark stood there dumbfounded. His fear was showing. A User!!

The hideous image of the MCP twisted into an even more frightening shape. "Perhaps you'd rather take your chances with me?"

Suddenly, Sark felt the strength draining out of his body. The MCP cut off his power cycles. "No, wait!" he cried.

"I want him in the games until he is destroyed. Acknowledge?"

"I acknowledge! I—"

"End of line."

Flynn was led into a building and down a row of cells. "In here, program!" barked a guard, roughly shoving him through a door.

"Who are you calling 'program'? You're the program!" cried Flynn. Suddenly, he noticed his hands. They were glowing! Quickly, he looked himself over. From head to foot he was covered with—with what? It looked like armor . . . metal plates . . . circuitry!

Then all at once the truth dawned on him. "I'm a program!"

"Welcome to the pits," said a friendly voice through a little window in one of the walls. "My name is Ram."

"Hey?" asked Flynn, going up to him. "Would you like to do me a fantastic favor?"

"I can't break either of us out," said Ram sadly.

"Just answer a question. I'm in a jail for programs, right?"

"Right. You're a guest of the Master Control Program. They're going to make

you play video war games."

"Well, great!" Flynn sighed, vastly relieved. "For a moment there I was worried. But I play video games better than anybody."

"You're lucky then!" shouted a guard as all the cell doors flew open. "Because everybody's going up on the game grid. Get moving!"

The guards herded the prisoners out into the open and onto a high ledge. Down below, stretching away as far as the eye could see, were the great game arenas.

"Hey, Ram," Flynn murmered so that the guards couldn't hear. "I know what I'm here for. But all these prisoners—what's their crime?"

"Where've you been?" Ram whispered back. "There's only one crime, and that's believing in the Users who wrote us. If we refuse to acknowledge the MCP's power, he takes over our functions and then shoves us into the games to have the bits blasted out of us."

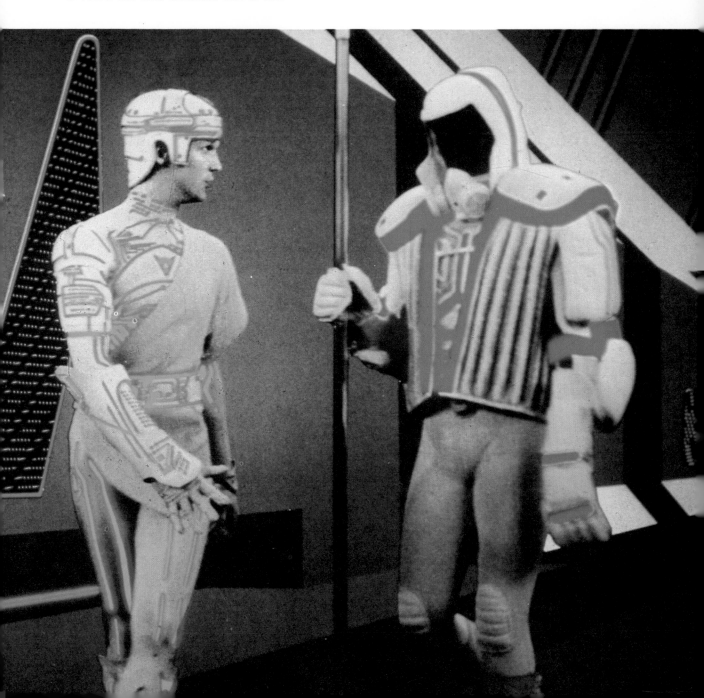

As they spoke, a great shadow fell over the grid. Flynn looked up. Hovering in the electronic sky was an enormous warship. There was something familiar about it, Flynn thought. All of a sudden, he remembered. It was the ship in one of the games in his arcade. A game that he himself had invented for ENCOM!

"Oh man!" he told himself. "It sure looked smaller from the outside."

"Look operative, you guys!" called a guard. "Command Program Sark will give you your instructions."

Stepping out on the bridge of the battleship, the huge red warrior stared down at them. "Greetings!" he boomed over the loudspeakers. "Listen closely. This is all the training you will get in the games, unless you desert your Users and come over to us! Anyone wishing to change his mind—let him do so *now*!"

Sark waited but no one spoke or moved. Now the warrior's hawklike eyes scanned the faces until they came to rest on Flynn. His hard, cruel mouth curled into a smile that was more like a snarl.

"You want mean and ugly?" Flynn said to himself. "Now *that's* mean and ugly. It reminds me of Dillinger."

"Very well," Sark continued. "You will each receive an identity disc. Everything you do or learn will be programmed on it. If you lose your disc or fail to follow orders, you will be put to death by de-resolution. That is all."

As the guards headed them back to their cells, they passed above an arena where a game was going on. One lone prisoner, using his disc as a shield, held

off four of Sark's fiercest red fighters. The programs slowed down to gape. Even the guards stopped.

"Watch this guy!" said Ram.

Two red warriors suddenly hurled their discs at the same time. Moving swiftly, the blue defender blocked them both, then fired off his own. The hurtling disc connected! One of the red warriors staggered and nearly fell. The disc circled like a boomerang and snapped back into the blue warrior's upraised hand.

"Ain't he something?" said another prisoner. "One hundred and ten wins."

"How many losses?" asked Flynn.

The program looked at him strangely. "One loss and that's all she wrote."

"Some world you got here," muttered Flynn to himself.

Circling around their opponent, the reds felt that they had him cornered. "Waste him!" one of them screamed, and all four let loose at once.

The blue warrior leaned to the side and threw. It was a clear hit! One program down! The disc flew back to him. He whirled and threw again. Another warrior was shattered. The third saw it coming and held up his shield. But the disc whizzed past him and hit the other red square in the stomach.

Only one red was left—the toughest one. He dug in, ready for anything. The blue warrior took careful aim and lashed out. The throw looked wild, spinning high and off to the side. Then, all of a sudden, it dipped, curved past the enemy's shield, and sliced into him. It was all over!

"Who *is* that guy?" Flynn asked Ram quickly.

The program brightened into a wide smile. "There's only one like him anywhere. Tron!"

"TRON?" cried Flynn. "I have to talk to him."

"Silence," shouted a guard, grabbing hold of him.

"Wait!" boomed Sark from the bridge. "Let that one fight right now." Then a cruel chuckle came into his voice. "Only let him fight one of his *own* kind— another prisoner program. Take him to the rings."

Pulling another prisoner out of the crowd, the guards led each of them onto a different round platform hanging in space. Flynn looked at the long-handled net that appeared in his hand and suddenly remembered the game. It was the one that boy had been playing in his arcade. The thought made him laugh.

This offended the other prisoner. "Oh, so you think I'm just a joke, huh?" he called out nervously. "Because all I ever did before was help a bank manager figure out mortgage payments. But *you're* some kind of a tough guy!"

"No! That's not it," said Flynn. "We're in the same boat and—"

The frightened program didn't wait to listen. He flung an energy pellet with all his strength. It bounced off another platform floating above their heads, then zoomed straight at Flynn.

Flynn lunged for it with his net. He missed. The ball sailed into one of the rings that made up his platform. The ring broke away at his feet, and Flynn lost his balance at the very edge!

Another pellet came hurtling at him. Flynn leaped away from the edge, caught the ball, and threw it. It hit! And a ring vanished from his opponent's platform.

"Now that's more like it!" shouted Flynn. Having tasted the excitement of the contest, he forgot all about its being a matter of life and death. One ring after another fell away from the feet of the other program before Flynn noticed stark terror in the face across from him.

"Here's an easy one," he said, lobbing a ball.

But it was no use. The shaken prisoner missed even that one. It crashed into the ring that he stood on. He began to fall, but desperately grabbed hold of the last remaining ring.

Flynn had the pellet now, ready to throw. But he didn't move.

Sark's huge image appeared on the front of the overhead platform. "Finish the game!" he roared. "Kill him!"

"Forget it!" shouted Flynn, and he threw the pellet away.

Back in the real world, the game stopped.

"Hey! No fair!" screamed the kid in the arcade. "It's the same thing as last time—only worse! I want my money back. Where's Flynn?"

Sark was furious. He would not be disobeyed. The defeated program must die! He pressed a button on his computer console. The last ring dissolved under the hands of the dangling program, and he went plunging down...down...down.

But Sark wasn't satisfied. There was still a score to settle. "For defying me, User," he muttered to himself, "you can go right after him." He reached out to press another button, but the voice of his master sounded in his ears, "Only in the games! He is to die fighting only in the *games*."

Wrenching himself away from the button, Sark signaled the end of the game, and guards rushed up to Flynn. "Take him to game grid fourteen," their general commanded. "I'll get rid of him and that other pest at the same time!"

Flynn was boiling with anger over Sark's cruelty as the guards led him away. A red warrior strolled by and deliberately bumped into him. With one smooth motion, Flynn reached back for his disc. Even though Flynn was a prisoner, the red warrior took one look at his eyes and backed off quickly.

Flynn found himself in another game arena. He looked around. There's something familiar about this place, he thought.

The cycle grid! "They want to kill me with another game I made up," he told himself with a sigh.

"I hear you want to talk to me," said a voice behind him. He whirled around and found himself staring into the face of..."ALAN!"

Tron frowned. "How do you come to know my User's name?" he asked almost suspiciously.

"Your User?" Flynn stammered in confusion. "Well...uh...yeah...I'm a program from a User that knows Alan. The name is Flynn. *My* name, I mean."

"It's all right. Take it easy," said Ram, who was standing nearby. "Your memory will come back after a while. It happens to a lot of us when they first

pull us out of our regular computers and bring us here."

"Right...yeah," said Flynn, turning to Tron. "But a lot of stuff is coming back to me already. Like my User wants me to go after that MCP."

Tron stared even harder at this strange newcomer. Could this program be a police spy? he wondered. Ever since Tron was suddenly arrested, Sark and his guards had been trying to get information about his true functions.

Yet there was something about this program, Flynn. Something wild maybe, but something that he sensed he could trust. "That's what my User wants, too," he said at last.

"I know."

Tron and Ram stared at each other as if to ask themselves, "But *how* does he know?"

Suddenly, streams of electrons crackled around them. Handlebars formed, then whole motorcycles created out of pure light! Across the way, three enemy warriors on blue lightcycles geared up to go. A buzzer sounded, and the two teams roared off to battle.

As the warriors circled the arena to feel each other out, Flynn reminded himself how the game was played. The idea was to get the other guy to crash into a wall. The walls kept closing in because, wherever you rode, new walls came right up behind you. The open spaces got smaller and smaller until you had to —

Suddenly, the enemy's lead warrior and Tron raced straight at each other! It was a duel! Quickly, their cycles ate up the distance that separated them. Each rider was determined not to be the first one to pull away from the oncoming head-on crash. The gap closed.

"Turn! Turn!" Ram cried out.

But Tron plowed ahead until it was too late! But not quite! The onrushing cycles almost touched, then veered off together in the same direction.

They were safe, but only for the moment. The walls they had created behind them were closing in on Tron and his enemy. Now the warrior on the blue cycle, weaved and turned, trying to build a tight box of walls around Tron. But Tron on his gold cycle slipped out of the trap. "Ram!" he called into the mike. "Stay all the way over! Keep those walls away."

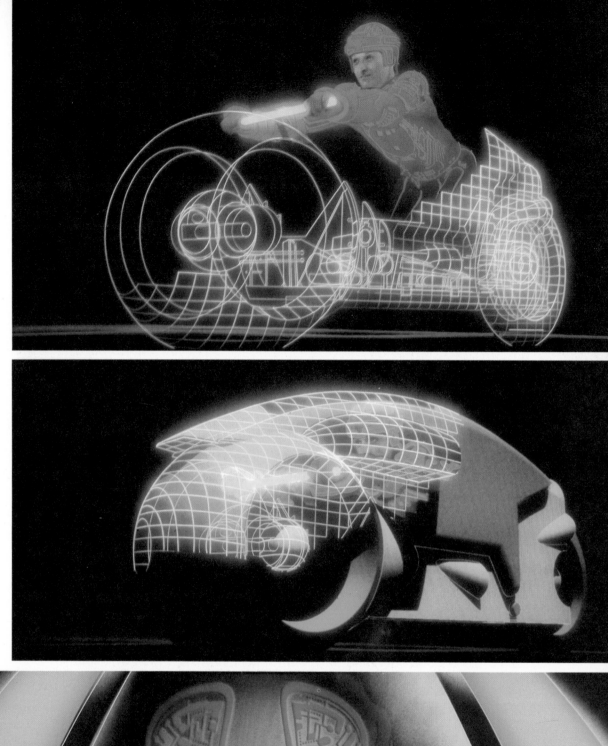

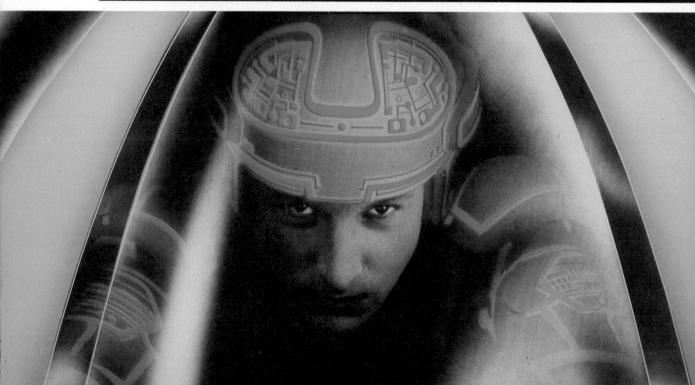

"I've got control. Go ahead!" Ram called back.

Tron rushed forward with his opponent right beside him. Ahead was one side of the arena. But next to the blue lightcycle was one of the new walls. Tron edged his enemy over to it. The blue cycle exploded and disappeared. As it did, all of the walls that the enemy warrior had created also vanished.

Flynn, too, was locked in battle with an enemy cyclist. Side by side, they raced along, turning this way and that as they tried to force each other to crash. But, all at once, Flynn spotted something very peculiar up ahead. It looked like a weakness in the construction of the arena itself. The explosion before had cracked open a thin hole in one of its sides! Forcing his opponent to the side, he headed them both straight for the permanent wall.

On his console screen, Sark watched the User head toward what he thought was certain death. His Dillinger-like lips curled into a hard, vicious smile as he watched the tremendous crash. He saw his own warrior and light-cycle disintegrate.

But what about the User? Sark gaped in astonishment. The User had escaped! And the other two prisoners were following him! Sark set off the alarms and ordered his tanks out.

Swarming from everywhere, the tanks closed in on the fleeing prisoners. They had them in their sights, but did not fire.

"Wait till they get clear of the game missile area!" cried a captain to his programs. "Or we'll blow it all up!"

Bursting onto a ramp, Flynn and the fleeing programs lost their protection. Weaving to avoid the bursting shells, they broke into wild canyon country. High rocklike pillars towered over them. Everywhere the ground curved and fell away below their wheels in sheer, dizzying drops. There was no chance of slowing down. The tanks were right behind them. The gunners were already getting their range. Only a miracle could save the three riders now.

Then a miracle happened. One tank, following too closely behind another, smacked into it and sent it toppling into a gorge. Taking advantage of the confusion, the three new friends slipped into the darkness of a cave and came to a stop. They waited in breathless suspense while the tanks lumbered by outside—and rolled on.

"Well," said Flynn after they had a little time to rest. "When do we pay a call on ol' Master Control?"

"What? Just the three of us?" Ram wondered aloud.

"Unless you know where we can rent an army, we're it," Flynn answered.

Tron had been thinking. "We can't even get to the MCP without help from Alan. There's a factory city on the other side of the canyons. If I can get to the input-output tower and get in touch with him . . ."

Leaving the safety of the cave, the trio began their ride toward the factory city. They made good time through the electronic landscape and finally came upon a bridge that led across the last canyon. A perfect place for an ambush, thought Tron. But there was nothing he could do about it. With himself in the lead, they raced for the other side.

"Fire!" cried the gunmen in the hidden tank. Its big cannon let loose. A screaming shell streaked through the sky and crashed into the bridge just in front of Flynn and Ram. Caught by the explosion, the two lightcycles reared back and disintegrated.

Tron was alone now. He had lost his friends! Soon other tanks appeared on his side of the wrecked bridge. He turned and rode off at top speed for a narrow gully . . . where he disappeared among the rocks.

Standing on the deck of his warship, Sark stared at the computer screen. "Good! That takes care of the User!" he told himself. "But that other trouble-maker is still out there. And if I don't stop him, the MCP will blast me into the

dead zone!" He gave orders for his command ship to head for the factory city immediately.

    For some moments, Flynn lay where he had fallen. Slowly, he regained his senses and struggled to his feet. Ram lay sprawled over a rock, wounded and unconscious. Flynn threw him over his shoulders. "Well, the bridge is gone," he said to himself. But there must be some other way out of these canyons. He set off.

    After a difficult walk, he found his way down from the mountain country. Exhausted, he looked for a place to hide for the night. Just ahead was a kind of junkyard. Stumbling around in the darkness, he found an opening in a big machine and carried the moaning Ram inside.

As he set the program down, Flynn's hand touched part of the wall. Suddenly, a blast of energy jumped out of him, and the whole machine began to rumble and shake. "What's going on here?" he exclaimed.

"We're inside a Recognizer," whispered Ram weakly.

"Hey! A robot! Something that *moves*!" Standing up, Flynn threw his arms out wide, and the gigantic robot rose up on its feet!

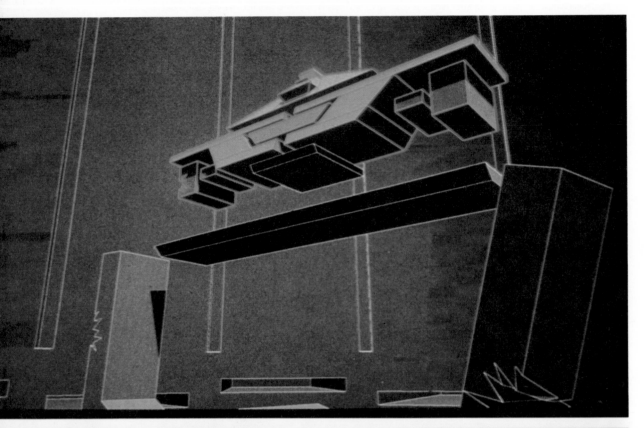

But Ram was dying. "Tell me who you really are?" he pleaded when Flynn rushed to his side.

"Flynn. Just Flynn. I told you."

"No," Ram gasped. "A program couldn't do what you did." He took Flynn's hands in his. "You've got to help Tron. Help . . . Tron."

Flynn looked on in great sorrow while the dying program gave up his last bit of energy and vanished.

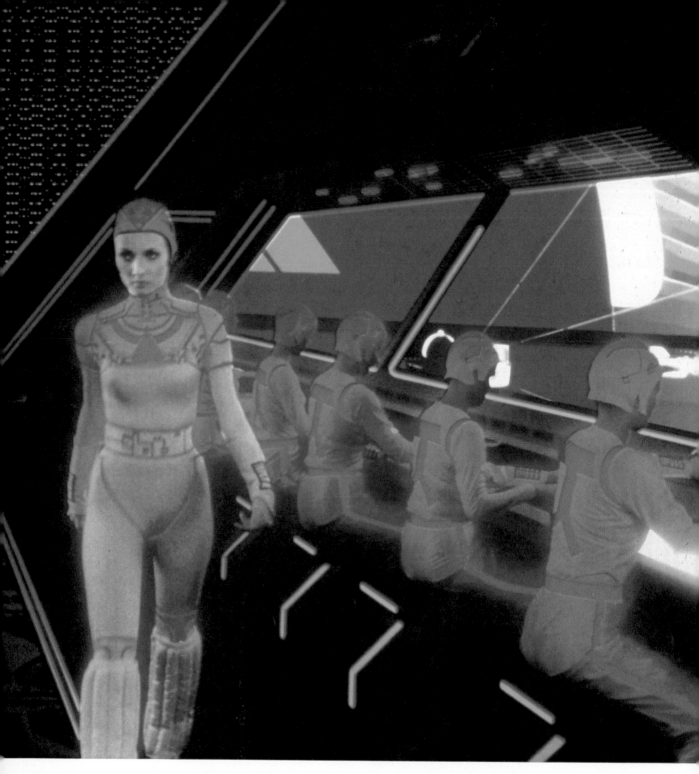

Arriving in the factory city, Tron was amazed by what he saw. The buildings were turned into faded ghosts of themselves. Even the programs walked the streets with dull, unseeing eyes, muttering nothing but numbers. Suddenly, he realized what had happend. The whole city had been drained of its energy. The MCP was killing it off!

Tron thought of his girlfriend Yori. She, too, could be slowly dying. Her factory was nearby. Racing into it, he made his way to a computer control room in the game building unit. It overlooked a vast hanger where a video game sailing ship was being put together electronically.

Sure enough, Yori was working. He waited until a guard had passed and

drew her off behind a pillar. But she gazed at him with eyes that didn't see him —like a sleepwalker!

Taking her in his arms, he held her until his own energy passed into her and brought her back.

"Oh, Tron!" she cried. "I knew you'd escape!"

Quickly, he told her what had happened. "Yori, can you get me to the input-output tower so that I can reach Alan?"

"Not yet. Tonight. Then Dumont, the Keeper of the Light, will be alone." A guard appeared nearby and walked toward them. "Come with me!" she said, taking his hand. "I'll hide you till then."

Flynn was having problems steering the Recognizer. And the little glow of light that kept darting around all over the place wasn't helping much.

"Okay," he called out at last. "Hold it right there."

"Yes!" cried the little glow, widening into a green ball, then falling back into light again.

"What do you mean, 'Yes'?"

"Yes. *Yes*. Yes! YES!"

"Is that all you can say?"

"No," it replied and turned red. "Uh-uh, nyet, no way..."

"Oh, anything else?"

"Yes! Da! Yesiree! Sure 'nuff! You betcha!"

"Only yes and no stuff, huh? Oh, I get it. You're a *Bit*!"

"For sure!"

"So, Bit, where's your program? Won't it miss you?"

But Flynn was a dead ringer for Clu. "No..." the Bit murmured, turning a very confused red.

"Wait a minute," said Flynn, catching on. *"I'm* your program?"

"Right on the money!" yelped the Bit in enthusiastic green.

"Another mouth to feed," sighed Flynn just as his Recognizer staggered into the city and smashed straight into a building. "I've got to stop this thing!" he shouted when it crashed again.

"Yes!" cried Bit as the robot's head tore off and went flying—with them in it. "I couldn't have put it—"

SPLAT!

Tron and Yori slipped unseen into the building where the tower was located. As they moved along swiftly, a guard loomed in front of them. Tron dropped him without a sound, and they rushed through a nearby door.

A vast hall was in front of them. Guards were everywhere. They ducked for cover, but it was too late—the alarm was sounded!

"This way!" whispered Yori. They raced off, but their path was blocked! *Now* what? Tron spotted an opening in the wall. He pulled Yori toward it. The guards rushed by without seeing them. He looked up. They were standing just outside an open airshaft. It rose straight up through the tower itself!

They caught hold of one of its dangling cables and started their perilous climb. Up, up, up they went to a dizzying height. At last, they climbed onto a narrow ledge.

"Look!" Yori cried, pointing to an open window. Edging carefully along the ledge, they peered down.

Inside, a hundred feet below, was Dumont, the Keeper of the Light. He sat, with eyes closed, upon a glowing platform.

A shout from the depths of the shaft startled Yori and Tron. Looking down, they saw a craft filled with armed guards. It was rising swiftly toward them.

"Let's go!" cried Tron.

Climbing through the window, they slid down the sloping wall into the chamber. Tron ran toward Dumont's platform, but its glowing heat drove him back.

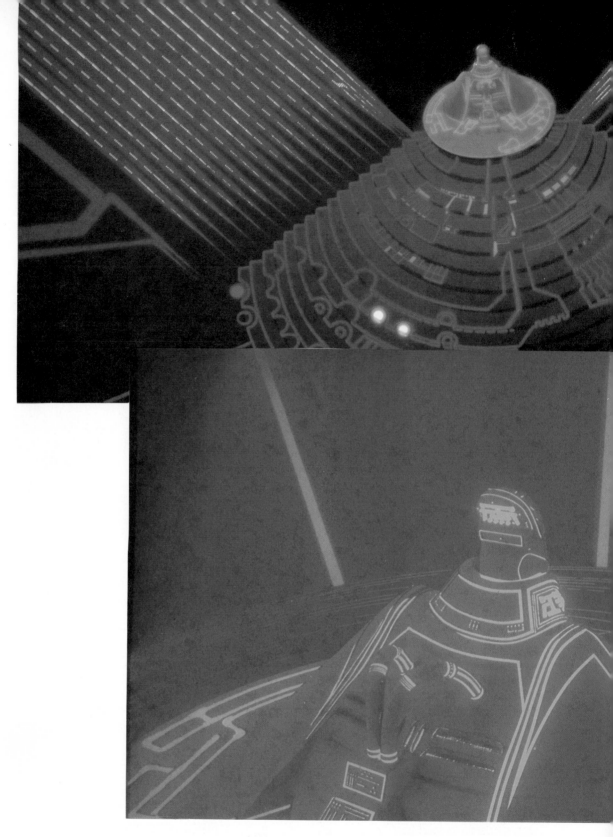

"Why do you disturb my peace?" growled Dumont, opening one eye. "What do you want?"

"To communicate with my User, Alan One. I...I can feel him calling me," Tron stammered, "and it's very...it's urgent!"

"Dumont!" said Yori, when the old program shook his head. "Tron's User has information that could free the whole System again!"

"Hah! A likely story!" grumbled Dumont. "Just good enough to get me

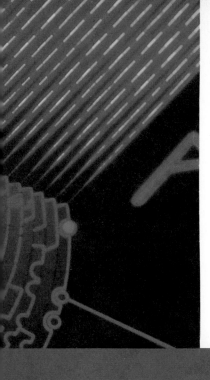

disintegrated. What are you pointing at?" Looking up, he saw the guards peering in at the high window. "Oh, all right. All right!" he muttered, and snapped it shut in their faces. He turned to Tron, still only half believing. "Just a moment," he said.

The platform's heat cooled. Tron sprang up the steps to the top and passed into the darkened opening beyond it.

Flynn dusted himself off and lost no time finding the tower. Sneaking inside with the Bit, he searched the building for his friend. The sound of many feet marching his way stopped him cold.

It was Sark leading his troops!

"So the tower guardian is helping Tron, is he?" snarled the general as he passed right under the ledge where Flynn had suddenly hidden himself.

The troops marched on—but with a slight change in the ranks. There was one warrior less, and Flynn was at the end of the line disguised in a new red glow.

"Bring in the logic probe," ordered Sark, stopping before Dumont's chamber door.

For the moment, Flynn could do nothing but watch as the needlelike machine floated past him and started to blast away.

Tron stood in the Communication Bell, holding his disc aloft. Silently, he awaited the moment of contact. At once, a golden beam of light burst down from the dome above. The disc, surrounded now by an unseen force, pulled free of his trembling hands, and rose into the light.

"TRON! TRON!" called an echoing voice from another world.

"Presence confirmed, Alan One!" cried Tron, happily.

"There you are! Look, before we get cut off again, I am going to give you some new coding. It will get you into the memory core of the Master Control..."

In the almost blinding light above, patterns formed. Dazzled by their beauty, Tron watched them change and move.

"When you get there," said Alan, in a voice growing fainter and fainter, "search out all the..."

"Wait! I can't hear you!"

But the voice was gone. Slowly, the disc returned to Tron. It had a golden light of its own now, for it shone with new power.

"Hurry!" cried Yori. "They're breaking in!"

A moment later, Sark and his warriors stormed into the chamber. But they were too late!

"Where has he gone?" Sark roared into Dumont's face.

"Why, I really don't know what you mean," answered the brave old program as he blocked the passage.

"This way!" said Yori, getting her bearings while they ran. Hurrying down a maze of passages, they arrived at the hangar where the game ship was berthed.

"Can it get me to the MCP?" Tron asked as they climbed aboard.

"Yes. Over the Game Sea and right into the central computer."

"Yori! Get down!" he shouted and lashed out at a guard.

As others tried to swarm onto the ship, Yori rushed to the controls and activated the ship. A powerful beam of energy hit the sail and sent them rocketing out onto the sea. They were on their way!

"Tron, look!"

A red warrior was clinging to the side. Tron raced up to the rail, ready to strike. A tiny ball of light streaked across his face, buzzing him like a bee. "No, sir!" it cried. "No way! Not on your life!"

"It's me, Flynn!" shouted the red warrior. "I surrender!"

Tron couldn't believe it. Flynn was alive. He pulled him to safety.

"Ram didn't make it," said Flynn. "I'm sorry, Tron." He stared at Yori. She was just as beautiful as her User, Lora.

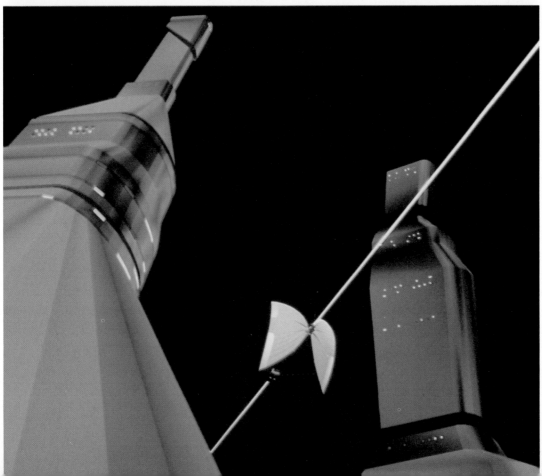

As their ship zoomed across the sea, Flynn confessed that he was a User from the other world. But he assured Tron and Yori that they were fighting together against the MCP.

"That's where we're headed," explained Tron. "Alan gave me the coding we need to go up against him."

"Well, all right!" Flynn cheered.

But things did not remain all right for long. Far away across the Game Sea, Master Control was aware of the growing danger. In less than a microsecond, his powerful mind raced over all the possible ways to put an end to his worries once and for all. Suddenly, he took action.

The solar sailer shook from top to bottom! Looking up, Tron saw that the transmission beam was going haywire. It was heating up!

"Power surge!" he cried. "We have to get onto another beam or we'll be cooked!"

Flynn pointed off to starboard. "I see one over there!"

"But we can't cross over!" called Yori from the controls. "There's no junction coming up!"

"Mama, say a prayer for your boy!" muttered Flynn under his breath as he rushed off for the bow. Before the horrified eyes of his two friends, Flynn threw himself face down into the path of the beam. As its tremendous charge of power passed through his body, he stayed conscious long enough to jut out one arm. A stream of energy blasted from his finger tips and bridged the gap to the other beam!

"He's *made* a junction!" exclaimed Tron. And the ship was guided to safety.

Flynn opened his eyes much later and saw Yori bending over him tenderly. He was thinking over whether or not to stay "sick" a while longer when the little crew got their next surprise: Sark!

His great command ship dove out of the sky without warning and plowed right into the solar sailer! *Crash!*

The smaller ship cracked apart. Desperately, Yori and Flynn grabbed for some wreckage to hold on to. "We've got to stay together or we'll be lost for sure," Flynn yelled.

But Tron, caught out in the open, was swept back from the bridge and fell overboard!

Flynn and Yori were scooped up by Sark's guards and taken to the brig of the warship. Old Dumont was among the prisoners already there. Bursting into tears, Yori rushed into his arms and cried, "Dumont, Tron is lost in the Game Sea! He's dead!"

Sark entered the brig with a look of triumph on his face. "Isn't this a touching scene," he sneered. But his grin vanished when he saw that Flynn was still alive. "Get the other prisoners on deck to be loaded into the shuttle craft," Sark ordered his guards. "Flynn and Yori, you will stay here and be deresolved with the rest of the ship," he said triumphantly.

Sark turned to look back at the doomed warship. It was already starting to fade into nothingness. "At last," he told himself, "I've finished them all."

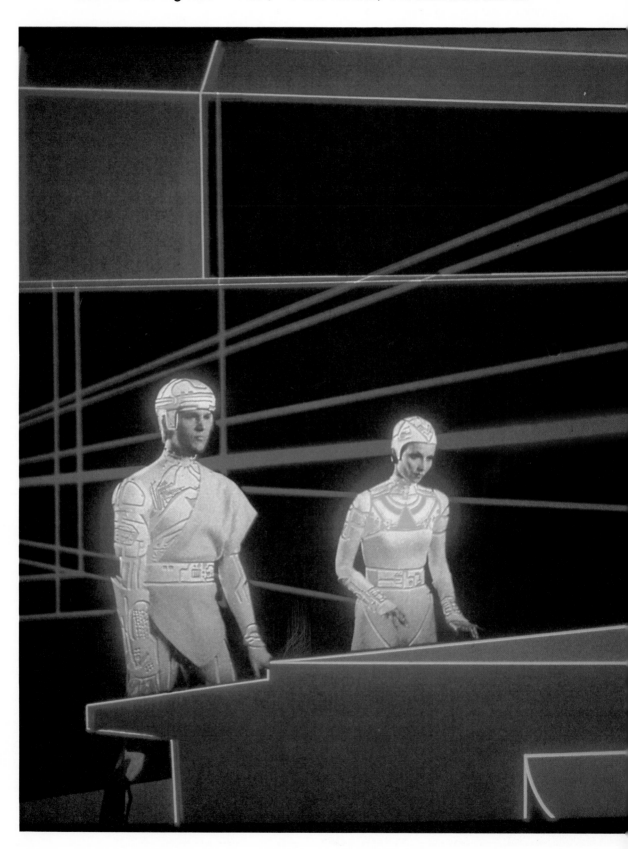

But Sark was wrong. For the craft that was rapidly taking him to the Master Control Program was also carrying an unexpected passenger. Outside, hang-

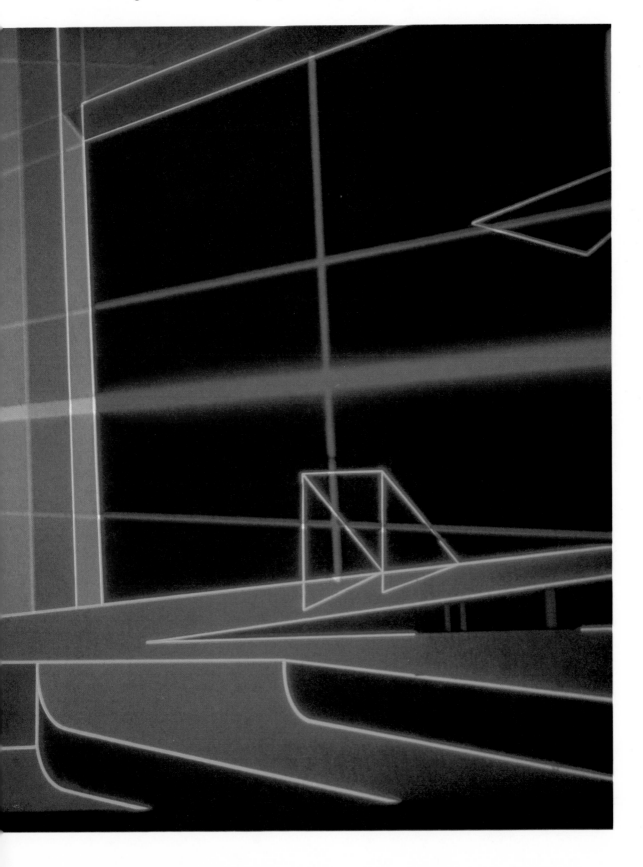

ing on tightly, was Tron!

Just before Sark landed, Tron dropped to the ground and ducked out of sight. Keeping in the shadows, he followed Sark and the prisoners to the towering cylinder of the MCP.

"Soon," MCP said to Sark from his tower, "only *I* shall be the contact with the other world. *I* who am the highest form of life in all worlds!" But suddenly, he stopped.

Tron stepped out of the shadows and called, "Sark!"

The huge warrior turned. The two enemies were face to face at last. Carefully, they stalked each other, their discs held ready. Suddenly, Sark threw. Quickly, Tron shielded himself and knocked it away. Then Tron threw his disc, but Sark knocked it down.

"We would have made a great team," sneered Sark as the battle raged. Neither was able to get the better of the other. "But you can't last much longer," Sark taunted him.

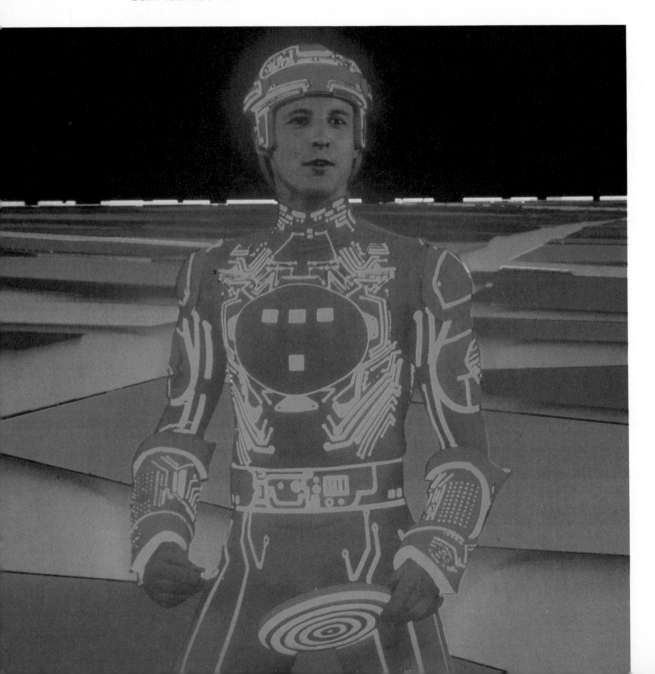

Just then Tron looked up, his attention caught by the approach of a ghostly, fading battleship. Sark saw his chance and hurled his disc. At the last split second, Tron leaped aside. Sark's disc sailed past Tron, then snapped back into the red warrior's hands. Tron regained his balance, set himself, and threw straight at Sark's shield. Tron's disc hit with an unbelievable force and cut right through Sark! The red warrior fell to the ground—dead at last!

The MCP's face on the cylinder seemed dazed, confused, and terrified. "You! Program! Stop!" it shrieked, as Tron walked into its central chamber with fire in his eyes. "I will not allow this! SARK, RISE! SARK, RISE!"

The dead warrior rose from the ground, half again as huge as he was before. He lurched toward Tron, a zombie under the MCP's control! The MCP's voice came from Sark's body. "Tron!" it called. "You're end of line, you program!" With its bare hands, it knocked aside Tron's flying disc. Tron seemed helpless before his foe.

Suddenly, from high above, a form jumped out of the fading warship straight into the energy beam of the MCP. It was Flynn, trying the only way he could think of to save his friend. The beam carried him into the head of the MCP itself! Flynn had turned himself into a human bullet!

The face on the cylinder was shaken. The zombie staggered. Quickly, Tron fired his disc—not at Sark—but high up into the center of the MCP's energy

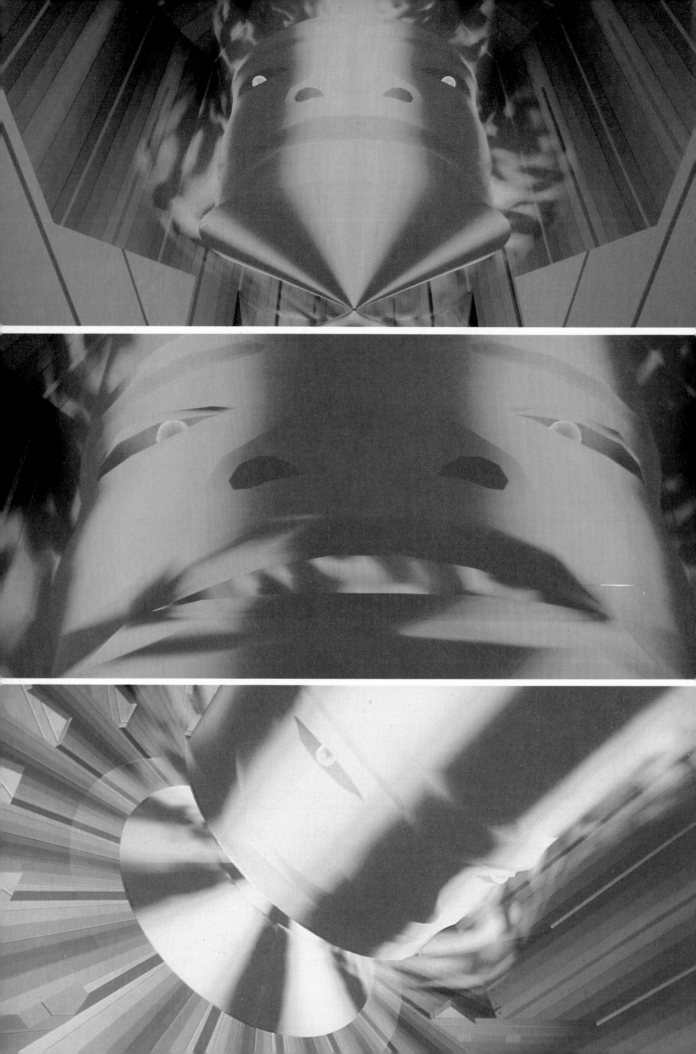

cone. *Boom!* The Master Control Program disintegrated into the black of space.

Yori steered what was left of the warship to the ground and rushed to Tron. "Where is Flynn?" she asked.

"He jumped into the MCP's beam. He saved you. He saved *all* of us."

But what had become of Flynn, they wondered. Could he possibly have survived this, too? He was, after all, a User.

The sky was beginning to clear. Tron and Yori gazed up at a beam of energy that stretched far away—beyond where the eyes of two programs could see.

It took Flynn a while to be sure of anything. The first thought that came to him was that he was still alive. The next thought was, where am I?

He looked around. It seemed like a place he had been before. The laser lab! He gazed down at himself—no armor, no glow. He was just Flynn. He was a human being again!

He turned and looked at the computer screen. The data from that hidden file—the proof he needed against Dillinger—was coming up!

Tearing it out of the printer, he rushed with the information into Alan's office. The MCP was finished forever. Now was the time to nail the man who had created it.